CONTENTS

Different OPINIONS

Most adults watch television, or TV, every day. They might watch the news in the morning or a favorite show at night. Some adults try to limit the time they spend in front of the TV, but they generally believe watching some television isn't bad for them.

Many people have a different opinion about kids and television. They believe television is bad for kids and can lead to problems with learning, **behavior**, and health. However, other people believe television can be good for kids. These opinions can **affect** the rules adults make about how much and what kinds of television kids can watch.

Know the Facts!

The average American family watches almost 8 hours of television each day.

POINTS OF VIEW

Is TELEVISION Bad for Kids?

By Katie Kawa

KidHaven PUBLISHING

Published in 2020 by
KidHaven Publishing, an Imprint of Greenhaven Publishing, LLC
353 3rd Avenue
Suite 255
New York, NY 10010

Designer: Deanna Paternostro
Editor: Katie Kawa

Photo credits: Cover Syda Productions/Shutterstock.com; p. 5 (top) imtmphoto/Shutterstock.com; p. 5 (bottom) Pixel-Shot/Shutterstock.com; p. 7 (top-left) OHishiapply/Shutterstock.com; p. 7 (top-right) Andrey_Popov/Shutterstock.com; p. 7 (bottom) tenenbaum/Shutterstock.com; p. 9 (top) Jack Frog/Shutterstock.com; p. 9 (bottom) LightField Studios/Shutterstock.com; p. 11 (main) Sitthipong Pengjan/Shutterstock.com; p. 11 (inset) Andrew H. Walker/Getty Images; p. 13 eelnosiva/Shutterstock.com; p. 15 wavebreakmedia/Shutterstock.com; p. 17 Piotr Wawrzyniuk/Shutterstock.com; pp. 19, 21 (inset, left) Monkey Business Images/Shutterstock.com; p. 21 (notepad) ESB Professional/Shutterstock.com; p. 21 (markers) Kucher Serhii/Shutterstock.com; p. 21 (photo frame) FARBAI/iStock/Thinkstock; p. 21 (inset, middle-left) stockfour/Shutterstock.com; p. 21 (inset, middle-right) Africa Studio/Shutterstock.com; p. 21 (inset, right) Alena Ozerova/Shutterstock.com.

Library of Congress Cataloging-in-Publication Data

Names: Kawa, Katie, author.
Title: Is television bad for kids? / Katie Kawa.
Description: New York : KidHaven Publishing, [2020] | Series: Points of view | Includes index.
Identifiers: LCCN 2019009394 (print) | LCCN 2019011836 (ebook) | ISBN 9781534531987 (eBook) | ISBN 9781534531925 (library bound book) | ISBN 9781534532045 (pbk. book) | ISBN 9781534532106 (6 pack)
Subjects: LCSH: Television and children–Juvenile literature.
Classification: LCC HQ784.T4 (ebook) | LCC HQ784.T4 K365 2020 (print) | DDC 302.23/45083–dc23
LC record available at https://lccn.loc.gov/2019009394

Printed in the United States of America

CPSIA compliance information: Batch #BW20KL: For further information contact Greenhaven Publishing LLC, New York, New York at 1-844-317-7404.

Do you think television is bad for kids? It's important to learn all the facts about this issue so you can have an informed, or educated, opinion. If you think television is good for kids because you like watching television, that's an opinion, but it's not an informed one.

Screen TIME

Today, many adults aren't just worried about their kids watching too much television. They're also worried about them looking at any screen for too long. Watching television makes up a big part of screen time—the amount of time people spend looking at screens. However, screen time also includes playing video games and using computers, smartphones, and tablets.

Doctors have said that children between the ages of 2 and 5 should only have an hour of screen time each day. After kids reach the age of 5, their parents or guardians should decide how much screen time—including TV time—is right for them.

Know the Facts!

Many screens, including TV screens, give off a kind of light called blue light. Looking at screens that give off blue light can make it hard to fall asleep. This is why doctors believe people should stop looking at screens at least an hour before they go to bed.

A major study of kids and screen time was done in 2017. It showed that kids 8 years old and younger spent more than 2 hours looking at screens every day. Kids between the ages of 8 and 12 looked at screens for more than 4 hours every day.

Healthier CHOICES

One of the main reasons people believe in setting limits on screen time, including time spent watching television, is because it often takes the place of other activities that they believe are healthier and better for kids. For example, time spent watching television could be spent studying or doing homework.

Watching television is an activity that's often done sitting or lying down. Some people believe this is bad for kids' health because when they're watching television, they're often not being active. They think kids should use their free time to play outside instead of watching television.

Know the Facts!

More than half of all middle school students don't get enough sleep, which can cause health problems. **Experts** believe watching TV before bed is one reason kids don't get enough sleep.

Childhood **obesity** is a big problem in the United States, and people are looking for ways to help kids be healthier. Many people believe one way to help is to **encourage** kids to play and be active instead of watching television.

A Teaching TOOL

Although some people believe watching television takes away time kids can spend learning, other people believe the opposite can be true. They believe television can help kids learn new things.

Educational TV shows for young kids teach them important things such as letters and numbers. As kids get older, they can watch shows about science **topics** such as animals and nature. They can also watch shows that teach them about different places and different ways of life. If adults carefully choose the shows their kids watch, kids can learn a lot from television!

Know the Facts!

One of the oldest and most popular educational television shows for kids is *Sesame Street*. Its first **episode** aired in 1969, and it's still teaching kids about math, reading, friendship, and kindness today.

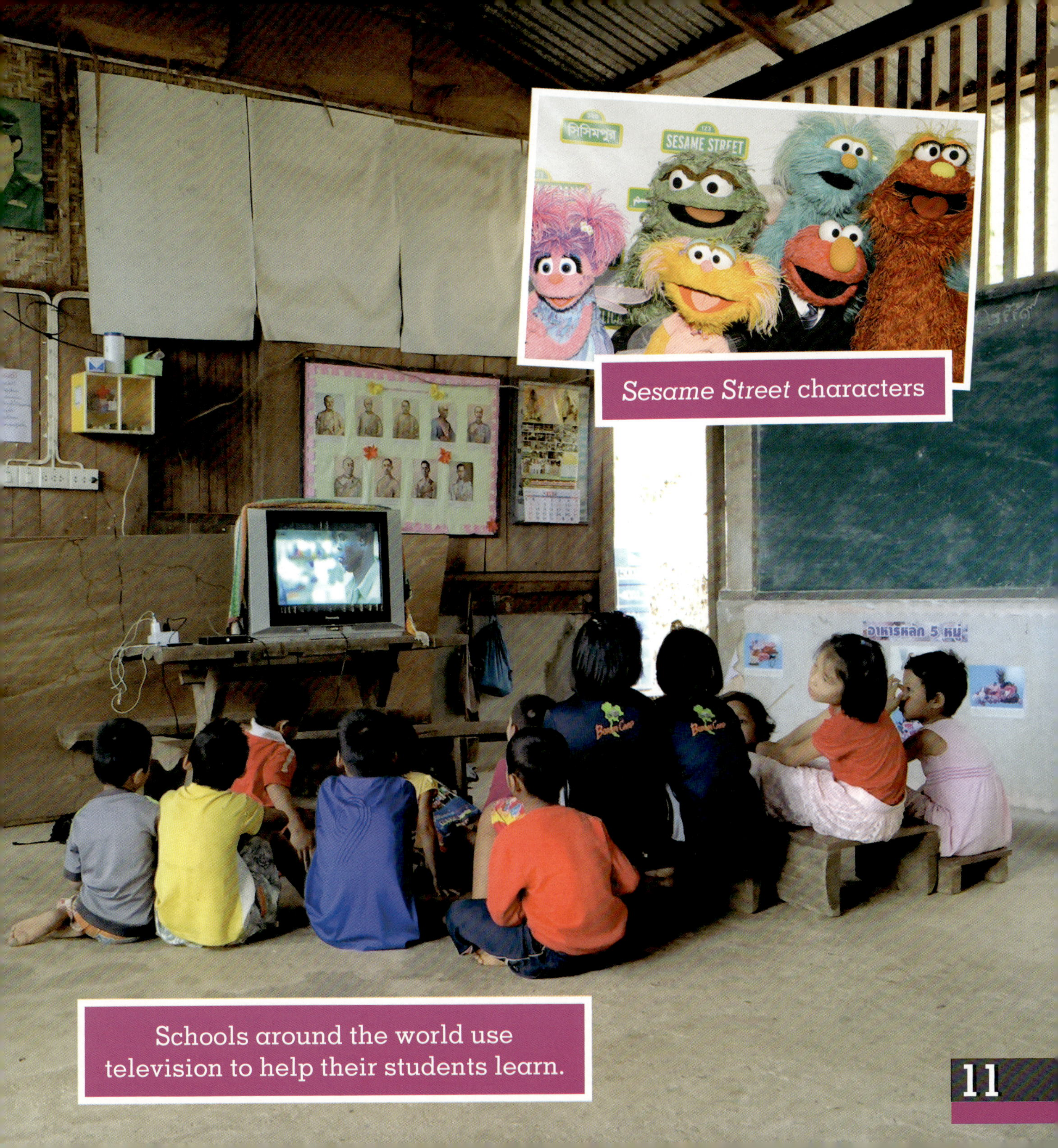

Sesame Street characters

Schools around the world use television to help their students learn.

Not for ALL AGES

Most people believe that educational TV shows aren't bad for kids. However, many kids—especially kids who are allowed to choose what they watch—aren't watching educational television all the time. Instead, they're watching shows that don't teach them anything good—and sometimes teach them bad things.

Some TV characters act in ways that set a bad example for kids. They use bad language, are mean to others, and sometimes use **violence**. Many adults worry that watching too much violence on television can be harmful for kids.

Know the Facts!

Studies have shown that seeing violence on television can cause children to be more aggressive, or ready to attack others. It can also cause children to see violence as a common part of life, which isn't healthy.

Adults can sometimes set special controls that allow them to choose what TV shows their kids can watch. Many people believe this is a good idea because most TV shows aren't made for kids and can often scare them.

Good EXAMPLES

Some TV characters set a bad example for kids. However, there are also many TV characters who are good role models—people for kids to look up to. For example, many TV shows today feature women who are smart, successful, and strong. This helps both boys and girls grow up to believe that women and men should be treated as equals.

TV shows made for kids and families often tell stories about how kids can handle problems at school and home in healthy, positive ways. This sets a good example for kids who are watching.

Know the Facts!

Experts believe some TV shows help people **develop** empathy, which is the ability to understand another person and to feel what they're feeling. When people have a strong sense of empathy, they treat others with more kindness.

Some TV shows are about African American families. Others feature characters who come from different countries or who have a disability. If these TV shows are written well, they can help kids better understand themselves and people who are different from them.

Commercials AND KIDS

TV shows aren't the only things people watch when they're watching television. They also see advertisements called commercials, which are created to make people want to spend money on a good or service.

Many commercials are for junk foods, such as cookies, soda, or candy, and fast food restaurants. Kids are strongly affected by advertisements, so they often make choices based on the commercials they see. This can lead to them eating more junk food, which harms their health. In fact, some studies have shown a connection between watching commercials and childhood obesity.

Know the Facts!

Some advertisements are created to make girls and women believe they'll be prettier and happier if they buy and use a certain product. Experts believe these kinds of advertisements cause girls and women to feel bad about themselves.

Many people argue that television is bad for kids because it leads to bad eating habits. For example, when people see commercials for unhealthy foods, they're more likely to eat those unhealthy foods while watching television.

Something to TALK ABOUT

Parents and guardians can do their part to help lessen the effects of advertisements by talking to their kids about how commercials work. They can also talk to them about other things they see on television and how they feel about what they're watching.

Television can help adults teach their kids important life skills. One of these skills is **media literacy**. Someone with strong media literacy skills is able to think deeply about a TV show and how it affects their thoughts, actions, and feelings. This can help them make smart choices about what TV shows they watch.

Know the Facts!

A 2017 study showed that kids who watch TV with their parents were more likely to learn from what they were watching than kids who watched TV alone.

Watching television can be a good way for families to spend time together and to learn about each other. Sometimes talking about a TV show can help parents and kids start talking about problems at home or at school.

Making Smart CHOICES

Is television bad for kids? After learning the arguments and facts on both sides of this **debate**, you can see that's not an easy question to answer. Some TV shows and commercials are clearly bad for kids. However, there are also many TV shows that can teach kids **valuable** lessons.

Making smart choices when watching television is important. Talk to trusted adults about what you're watching, and use your media literacy skills to think about how it affects you. This can help you form your own educated opinions about television.

Know the Facts!

In 2018, the results of a study by the U.S. government showed that watching television is Americans' favorite thing to do with their free time. In fact, Americans spend more than half of their free time every day watching TV!

Is television bad for kids?

YES

- Watching television can take the place of other activities that are healthier for kids, such as playing outside and sleeping.
- Many TV shows set a bad example for kids.
- Seeing violence on television can make kids more aggressive and can scare them.
- Advertisements on television can cause kids to eat more junk food or to feel bad about themselves.

NO

- Kids can learn important things from educational TV shows.
- Many TV shows provide kids with good role models.
- Television can help kids develop empathy and understand people who are different from them.
- Watching and talking about TV as a family can teach important life skills and help adults and children learn more about each other.

When it's hard to decide who you agree with in a debate, it can be helpful to make a chart such as this one to break down both sides.

GLOSSARY

affect: To produce an effect on something.

behavior: The way a person acts.

debate: An argument or discussion about an issue, generally between two sides.

develop: To create over time.

encourage: To make someone more likely to do something.

episode: One part in a series of connected stories.

expert: Someone who has a special skill or knowledge.

media literacy: The ability to find, think deeply about, and use different ways of communication that can inform a large number of people.

obesity: The condition of being very overweight.

topic: A subject people talk or write about.

valuable: Having great worth or importance.

violence: The use of force to harm someone.

For More INFORMATION

WEBSITES

BrainPOP: Media Literacy
www.brainpop.com/english/studyandreadingskills/medialiteracy
The videos, activities, and quizzes on this website can help you develop your media literacy skills.

Common Sense Media: Best TV for Kids
www.commonsensemedia.org/tv-lists
This website features lists of TV shows that are good for kids to watch, which can be broken down by different age groups—from preschoolers to teens.

BOOKS

Chagollan, Samantha, and Erika Milvy. *101 TV Shows to See Before You Grow Up*. Lake Forest, CA: Walter Foster Jr., 2017.

Picou, Lin. *TV, Yes or No*. Vero Beach, FL: Rourke Educational Media, 2016.

Weil, Jamie. *Asking Questions About What's on Television*. Ann Arbor, MI: Cherry Lake Publishing, 2016.

Publisher's note to educators and parents: Our editors have carefully reviewed these websites to ensure that they are suitable for students. Many websites change frequently, however, and we cannot guarantee that a site's future contents will continue to meet our high standards of quality and educational value. Be advised that students should be closely supervised whenever they access the Internet.

INDEX